The Berenstain Bears
and
TOO MUCH VACATION

Can a bear's vacation
with more rain than sun
end up being
the one that's most fun?

A First Time Book®

The Berenstain Bears and

Random House 🏠 New York

Library of Congress Cataloging-in-Publication Data:
Berenstain, Stan. The Berenstain bears and too much vacation. (A First time book) SUMMARY: The Bear family experiences one mishap after another when they vacation in the Great Grizzly Mountains. [1. Vacations—Fiction. 2. Bears—Fiction] I. Berenstain, Jan. II. Title. III. Series: Berenstain, Stan. First time books. PZ7.B4483Bemc 1989 [E] 88-32094 ISBN: 0-394-83014-8 (pbk.); 0-394-93014-2 (lib. bdg.)

Manufactured in the United States of America 1 2 3 4 5 6 7 8 9 0

TOO MUCH VACATION

Stan & Jan Berenstain

"Well, that's everything," said Mama Bear as she and Sister and Brother Bear held the car trunk lid so that Papa Bear could tie it down.

"Not quite," said Papa, running back into the tree house. "We almost forgot the camera," he said when he reappeared. "What good is a wonderful vacation without photographs to remember it by?"

"Good thinking, Papa," said Brother. "May
I take some pictures when we get there?"
"And how about me?" Sister wanted to know.
"Of course you may," said Papa as they
bundled into the car. "We're all going to
take pictures of the most wonderful vacation
the Bear family has ever had.
All right, now—everybody buckle
up and we'll be on our way!"

Four safety belts clicked into place
and they left their safe, comfortable
tree house and headed for the
excitement and adventure of a
vacation high up in the wilds
of the Great Grizzly Mountains.

It had been Papa's idea to take their vacation in the Great Grizzlies. "It'll be a real wilderness experience. We'll live off the land. We're getting too soft here in the valley with all our supermarkets and other conveniences."

When he saw the ad in the newspaper, there was no holding him. It said, "Try a Wilderness Vacation! A lovely mountain cabin complete with a rowboat by beautiful Crystal Lake!"

"Ah," said Papa, painting beautiful word pictures, "to wake with the rising sun and catch our breakfast from a clear mountain lake!

It all sounded great to the cubs. "What kind of fish will we catch, Papa?" asked Brother.

"Trout, no doubt," he answered with supreme confidence. But Mama wasn't so sure he would catch anything. So when she packed, she took along some canned goods in case the trout weren't biting, and some books and games in case of a rainy day.

"I can almost taste that fresh-caught trout," said Brother as the road led ever higher into the mountain forest.

"And I can almost taste those yummy wild berries," said Sister.

"And don't forget my terrific wilderness stew!" said Papa as he turned onto an even steeper road.

"But we didn't bring things for stew," objected Mama. "All we brought are some canned goods."

"Of course we didn't," laughed Papa. "I'm talking about my special live-off-the-land survival stew. It's my secret recipe. I make it from bark, leaves, and roots that I find in the woods."

"When will we get there?" asked
the cubs.
"Very soon. I can tell by the smell
of that mountain air," said Papa,
taking a deep breath.

"That's not mountain air," complained Brother, making a face. "That's skunk!"

"Hmmm," said Papa, wrinkling his nose.

A good time to start taking those pictures, thought Mama.

"Pew!" said Papa.

"*Click!*" said the camera.

"There's the cabin!"
shouted Sister as they
rounded a bend.

And there it was indeed—a mountain cabin beside a lake, complete with rowboat. Of course, it wasn't *quite* as they had pictured it from the ad. Crystal Lake looked more like mud soup. The lovely mountain cabin looked more like a tumble-down shack. There was a rowboat, all right, but it was half sunk in the lake.

But Papa wasn't the least bit discouraged. He was more excited than ever. "It's perfect!" he shouted. "The most perfect live-off-the-land vacation spot I've ever seen!" Mama wasn't so sure. She noticed that there were no wires leading into the cabin, which meant there was no electricity.

"That's the last thing we need," scoffed Papa. "What you need on a live-off-the-land vacation is plenty of can-do spirit and lots of forest smarts, and I've got enough of those for all of us."

He took a cooking pot and a folding chair from the car trunk. "Here," he said, making a seat for Mama. "This is a vacation. You relax while I gather the fixings for my fabulous wilderness stew.

"And you two tidy up the cabin," he called to the cubs as he headed into the forest with the cooking pot.

But Mama didn't expect to do much relaxing on this vacation, and she wasn't surprised to find that the cabin was an even worse mess inside than it was outside. There was an ankle-deep carpet of twigs, branches, and dead leaves on the floor, and it was practically a museum of spider webs, cocoons, and mouse nests.

Time for another picture, thought Mama. Scurry, scurry went the mice. *Click* went the camera.

"What's this?" asked Sister as she cleaned leaves out of the sink.

"That's a hand pump for water," answered Mama.

"Just what I need!" It was Papa, back with his cooking pot full of strange-looking bark, leaves, and roots. "A little water for my stew!" He worked the handle. The pump gurgled and squeaked and after a while began to squirt water—rusty brown water. But he wasn't discouraged. "Just what I need for my stew," he said cheerfully, "ready-made gravy!"

He carried the pot outside, where he had prepared a cooking fire. It was very exciting for the cubs. But Mama wasn't so sure. So she made a fire in the fireplace and warmed up a supper of canned beans and dried honeycomb.

When Papa cried, "Stew time!" the cubs ran out for a first taste. Mama followed with the camera.

"Here's to living off the land!" said Papa, holding up a big spoon of the strange-looking stuff. Then he, Brother, and Sister each took a taste.

"Yugh!" said Sister.
"Blech!" said Brother.
"P-tooey!" said Papa.
"*Click!*" said the camera.

Mama Bear's supper of beans and honeycomb proved very tasty. Papa Bear stretched and yawned.

"Now, early to bed so I can get up with the sun and catch our breakfast."

WHOOO! RIBIT RIBIT WHOO WHOO RIBIT RIBIT RIBIT CLICK CLICK WHOO RIBIT WHOO CLICK CLICK WHOO HOOT RIBIT RIBIT RIBIT

The sun did rise and it was very beautiful, but Papa snored right through it. The frogs, crickets, and owls had made such a racket during the night that he hadn't fallen asleep until just before the rising sun lit up the sky.

Papa began to get a *little* discouraged when he went out to catch breakfast. The boat sank as soon as he stepped into it, and all he caught was a gloppy mudsucker that made snuffling noises and stared.

"Snuffle, snuffle, glop," said the mudsucker.

"*Click!*" said the camera.

It was Papa's turn to snap the picture when Mama and the cubs tasted the wild berries. The thorns were something fierce and the berries were so sour even the birds puckered.

Later, there *was* a perfectly beautiful sunset.
But the Bear family didn't get to see much of it.
They were too busy swatting the swarms of hungry
mountain mosquitoes that swooped in from the lake.

"Live off the land, you say!" shouted Mama as
they ran for the cabin. "With all these thorns
and mosquitoes, it's more like the land
is living off us!"

It began to rain just as they reached the cabin. But the roof leaked badly, and pretty soon they had more leaks than they had pots and pans. They spent a miserable night.

By morning, they were soaked to their fur and there was a foot of water in the front stairwell.

"Don't worry," said Papa. "The rain can't last forever, and just as soon as I sweep out this water..." But instead of Papa sweeping the water, the water swept Papa—out the door, down the muddy slope, and into the muddy, mucky lake. When Mama and the cubs reached him, he looked more like a mud ball than Papa Bear.

"Say," he said, looking up at them. "I have a terrific idea—let's go home."

So the Bear family loaded the trunk, put the car top up, bundled into the car, and bumped and splashed down the mountain in the driving rain. The rain had stopped and the sun had come out by the time they reached the valley, and their tree house had never looked so good to them as it did that day.

The next day, Mama took the film to the camera store to be developed. When the pictures came back a few days later, the Bear family wrote titles on them. They began to chuckle as they passed the pictures around. The chuckles grew to roaring laughter, and soon they were laughing so hard they cried.

Papa smells the mountain air

We are greeted upon our arrival

We taste Papa's
Wilderness Stew

Papa catches
our breakfast

Our first taste of
wild mountain berries

Papa decides it's
time to go home

And every so often, through the years, they take out those pictures and have an absolutely wonderful time enjoying the worst vacation the Bear family ever had.